Five reasons why you'll love Isadora Moon...

Meet the magical,
fang-tastic Isadora Moon!

Isadora's cuddly toy, Pink Rabbit,
has been magicked to life!

Have you ever tried
ballet dancing?

Isadora's family is crazy!

Enchanting
pink and black
pictures

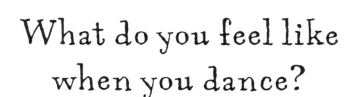

What do you feel like when you dance?

I feel I'm getting my grooves.
– Frankie

A bit shy, but happy too.
– Mae

When I jump I feel
like I'm flying.
– Sammy

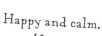

Happy and calm.
– Harriet

I feel a bit dizzy
when I spin around.
– Charlie

I feel excited and fizzy inside.
– Riley

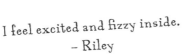

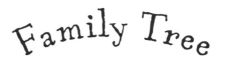
Family Tree

My Mum
Countess Cordelia
Moon

Baby Honeyblossom

My Dad
Count Bartholomew
Moon

Me!
Isadora Moon

Pink Rabbit

For vampires, fairies and humans everywhere!

And for Nicola, who loves the ballet.

OXFORD
UNIVERSITY PRESS

Great Clarendon Street, Oxford OX2 6DP

Oxford University Press is a department of the University of Oxford.
It furthers the University's objective of excellence in research, scholarship, and
education by publishing worldwide. Oxford is a registered trade mark of Oxford
University Press in the UK and in certain other countries

British Library Cataloguing in Publication Data

Data available

ISBN: 978-0-19-274437-1

5 7 9 10 8 6 4

Printed in Great Britain by Bell and Bain Ltd, Glasgow

Paper used in the production of this book is a natural,
recyclable product made from wood grown in sustainable forests.
The manufacturing process conforms to the environmental
regulations of the country of origin.

ISADORA ★ MOON

Goes to the Ballet

Harriet Muncaster

OXFORD
UNIVERSITY PRESS

Chapter ONE

Isadora Moon, that's me! And this is Pink Rabbit. He is my best friend. We do everything together. Some of our favourite things include: flying among the stars in the night sky, having glitter tea parties with my bat-patterned tea set, and practising our ballet.

9

We have been practising our ballet a lot recently and putting on shows for Mum and Dad. I have discovered that Dad's vampire cape makes a great stage curtain! It looks especially nice with silver-star sequins glued onto it . . . though I am not sure Dad agrees. He seemed a bit . . . annoyed last time he saw his best cape being used as a stage curtain.

'It's covered in stars!' he complained. 'I'm not a wizard, I'm a vampire! Vampires don't have starry capes.'

I felt a bit bad then but it was OK because Mum waved her wand and the stars all disappeared. She can do things like that because she's a fairy.

She was the one who magicked Pink
Rabbit alive for me.

'Good as new!' she said, sitting down
on one of the chairs Pink Rabbit and I had
put out for the audience. Dad sat down
too, with my baby sister, Honeyblossom,
on his lap, and they both waited for our
show to begin.

'Right,' I whispered to Pink Rabbit once we were behind the non-starry curtain. 'Can you remember your moves?'

Pink Rabbit nodded and did a perfect arabesque. He's been getting very good at ballet lately. I gave him a thumbs up.

'Let's go!' I whispered.

Together we leapt out from behind the curtain in a magnificent *grand jeté*. Mum and Dad clapped and cheered. Pink Rabbit began to pirouette on his tippy-toes. I swirled and twirled in my black glittering tutu.

'Marvellous!' called Dad.

'Enchanting!' said Mum, waving her

wand so that we were showered with pink
flower petals.

At the end of the show I gave a deep curtsey and Pink Rabbit bowed, and Mum and Dad cheered some more. Even Honeyblossom clapped her chubby little hands.

'That was really wonderful!' said Mum. 'And so professional!'

Pink Rabbit looked proud and puffed out his chest in his smart striped waistcoat.

'One day you'll both be prima ballerinas!' said Dad.

'I hope so!' I said as we both tiptoed gracefully across the floor, following Mum and Dad down the stairs and into the kitchen for breakfast. It was seven o'clock at night but we always have two breakfasts in our house. One in the morning and one in the evening. This is because Dad sleeps during the day. He has his breakfast in the evening before going out for his nightly fly.

'I want to be just like Tatiana Tutu!' I said as I began to spread a piece of toast with peanut butter. Tatiana Tutu is my favourite ballerina of all time.

I have never seen her in real life but I always watch the TV when she's on and I have a special scrapbook filled with pictures of her. I cut the pictures out of magazines and decorate them with starry sequins and silver glitter.

I also have a big poster of Tatiana Tutu on my bedroom wall. In it she is wearing a sparkling black tutu and her famous star diamond tiara. Her black tutu looks exactly like the sort a vampire fairy might wear . . . it looks just like mine!

'If you keep practising and work hard at your ballet I'm sure you'll be as good as Tatiana Tutu one day,' smiled Dad as he poured himself a glass of his red juice. Dad only ever drinks red juice. It's a vampire thing.

'Yes,' said Mum. 'Keep practising and one day maybe we'll come to watch you and Pink Rabbit perform in a real theatre!'

Pink Rabbit bounced up and down. His greatest wish is to dance on a real stage, even more so than me!

The next day at school I told my friends
all about the ballet show Pink Rabbit and
I put on for Mum and Dad.

'That sounds so much fun!' said Zoe.
'Can I come round and we can do it again?
I could wear my pink tutu and be the
sugar plum fairy!'

'And I could wear my white tutu and be a dancing snowflake,' said Samantha, dreamily.

'I'll be the hero of the show,' said Oliver, jumping in. 'I'll wear a mask and my black cape!'

'There could be an interval with refreshments,' suggested Bruno. 'We could hand round biscuits to the audience.'

'Or ice cream,' said Sashi. 'That's what you're supposed to have in the interval of a show.'

'I love ice cream!' yelled Zoe.

Just then Miss Cherry came into the room. Miss Cherry is our teacher at human school and she is lovely.

She doesn't mind that I am a vampire fairy, she treats me just the same as everyone else.

'Good morning, everyone,' she said, beaming round the classroom. 'I have some exciting news for you all today.' She started to hand out some letters, giving one to each person.

'We are going on a school trip,' she said. 'To see a show!'

'A show!' said Zoe. 'We were just talking about putting on a pretend show!'

'Well, here's your chance to see a real one,' said Miss Cherry. 'We are going to see the *Alice in Wonderland* ballet!'

I felt my heart start to beat fast. A ballet show! We were going to see a real ballet show!

'You need to take the letter home and get your parents to sign it,' said Miss Cherry. 'And we also need some parents to volunteer to help on the trip.'

'Will there be biscuits in the

interval?' called out Bruno.

'I expect there will be ice cream,' said Miss Cherry.

'I told you,' whispered Sashi.

'There will be quite a famous ballerina playing the part of the White Rabbit,' continued Miss Cherry. 'You might have heard of her if you are interested in ballet. She's called Tatiana Tutu.'

'Tatiana Tutu!' I shouted, jumping up from my chair.

Tatiana Tutu

The whole class turned round.

'Yes,' said Miss Cherry. 'You obviously know who she is, Isadora.'

'I do,' I said in a smaller voice, suddenly aware that everyone was staring at me. I sat down quickly, feeling my face go pink with embarrassment.

Pink Rabbit didn't seem embarrassed
at all. He did a little hop and wiggled
his ears. He was beside himself with
excitement that Tatiana Tutu was going
to play the part of the *rabbit*.

As soon as I got home I showed the
letter to Mum.

'You have to sign it!' I said. 'Quick!
Or I can't go on the school trip.'

'Hang on a second,' said Mum.
'Let me read it properly, Isadora. It says
here that they are in need of parents to
volunteer for the trip.'

'They are,' I said, starting to feel a bit
worried. 'But not you and Dad.'

'Why ever not?' asked Mum.

'We could volunteer! It would be good for us to get a bit more involved with your school activities.'

'It's in the daytime,' I said. 'Dad will be asleep.'

'That's true,' said Mum. 'What a shame!'

I didn't think it was a shame at all, in fact I felt quite relieved. But when Dad came down for breakfast that evening he seemed very interested in the trip.

'I will volunteer!' he said enthusiastically. 'I will make an exception! Hand me the pen!'

I held the pen behind my back.

'There's really no need for you both

to come . . .' I began.

But Mum swooped in with her wand
and put a magic tick in the 'volunteer' box.

'How exciting!' she said.

Chapter
TWO

On the morning of the trip I woke early.
But not as early as Pink Rabbit. He
was already up and bouncing around
the bedroom when I opened my eyes,
practising his *pliés* and pirouettes.

'Today's the day we see Tatiana
Tutu!' I said excitedly, hopping straight
out of bed and starting to get dressed.

I put on my smartest outfit and then picked up Pink Rabbit's little waistcoat.

'You must wear this,' I told him. 'It's important to look smart for the ballet.'

Pink Rabbit let me put the waistcoat on him and then we flew down the stairs to breakfast.

'Good morning,' said Mum, who was already up and busy feeding Honeyblossom her bottle of pink milk. 'I'm going to drop Honeyblossom off at the babysitter's in a minute,' she said. 'I'll meet you and Dad at the school. You can walk there with him.'

'OK,' I said as I started to eat my breakfast.

I watched Mum flit around the kitchen, packing all the baby things into a bag. Then she went into the hall and put Honeyblossom into her pram.

'See you soon, Isadora!' she called as she left the house.

I continued to sit at the table and eat my breakfast. It was very quiet without Mum and Honeyblossom.

'I hope Dad comes down soon,'
I said to Pink Rabbit. He twitched his
nose worriedly.

But Dad was nowhere to be seen.
An awful thought struck me.

'I hope he hasn't overslept,' I said,
'it's almost time to leave!' Together we
jumped down from the table and flew up
the stairs. I banged loudly on the door to
Mum and Dad's bedroom. There was no
answer. All I could hear was the sound of
someone snoring.

'Oh dear,' I whispered, pushing open
the door.

Dad was lying in bed with all the
curtains closed and his eye mask on.

He was fast asleep.

'Dad!' I shouted in a panic. 'Wake up!
We have to leave for the school trip!'

'Wha—' Dad jerked awake and sat
bolt upright in bed. He ripped off his eye
mask and stared frenziedly round the
room.

'The school trip,' I said. 'It's today!'

'Oh no!' wailed Dad in dismay.
'I've overslept.'

'It's OK,' I said. 'If you can get ready
in five minutes we will still be on time.'

'Five minutes!' said Dad, aghast.
'I can't get ready in *five minutes!*
It takes me half an hour just to do
my hair!'

I sighed. Vampires are very picky
about the way they look. They like to
always be perfectly sleek and groomed.

'Well, we can't be late and hold
everyone else up!' I told him sternly.

Pink Rabbit and I went back down
the stairs and I put on my smartest cape.

We waited by the door for five minutes
but Dad did not appear.

'Dad!' I shouted. 'It's time to go!'

'All right, all right, I'm coming,' he
grumbled, appearing at the top of the
stairs. He didn't look like my dad at all.
His hair was sticking up all over the place
and he was wearing a pair of odd socks.

'Honestly!' he complained as he made
his way down the stairs. 'What a time to
have to be awake!'

I opened the front door and the three of us stepped out into the frosty air. Together we walked along the garden path, through the gate, and down the road to school. We couldn't walk very fast because Dad kept stopping to peer in car windows.

'I've just got to comb this bit of hair,' he explained, 'and this bit too.'

At last an angry man wound down his car window and shouted at Dad to stop staring in at him and Dad jumped back in fright.

'I think I'll wait until we get to the school,' he said, putting his comb away.

Mum was already there when I arrived, wearing a bright pink hi-vis jacket. Miss Cherry was busy ticking names off a register.

'Marvellous!' she said, beaming round the room at everyone. 'We are all here!' She burrowed in her teacher's bag and came up with another bright pink hi-vis jacket.

She held it out towards Dad.

'You need to wear this, Mr Moon,' she said. 'It's so that the children can see where you are at all times. It's for health and safety.'

Dad looked horrified.

'I can't wear that,' he protested. 'It doesn't go with my outfit!'

'Don't be silly,' hissed Mum, 'Just put it on.'

Dad put the jacket on but he didn't look very happy about it.

'I look ridiculous,' he sniffed. 'Very un-vampirey.'

Miss Cherry put her clipboard away and clapped her hands for silence.

'Is everyone ready?' she asked.
'It's time to go!'

We all started to follow her towards
the door but I noticed that Dad was
going in the opposite direction.

'I've got to finish doing my hair,'
he explained. 'You all go on without me.

I'll catch you up! I won't be a minute!' He disappeared off to the bathroom while the rest of us followed Miss Cherry out of the school towards the train station in the middle of town. Everyone was excited, and the air was full of chattering. I felt especially excited because I had never been on a train before.

'I can't believe you've never been on a train!' said Zoe, who was walking next to me and holding Pink Rabbit's other paw. *'Everyone's* been on a train before!'

'Not me,' I told her. 'My family mostly fly everywhere.'

The train station was big and grey and noisy. The trains looked like giant metal caterpillars crawling up and down the tracks. Mum didn't seem too happy and her fairy wings started to droop a little bit.

'Where are the flowers?' she asked. 'Where are the forests? Where's all the lovely nature?'

She pointed her wand at a couple of empty grey hanging baskets which were fastened to the station wall. Bright pink flowers immediately sprouted out of them and cascaded over the sides.

'Much better,' said Mum, smiling.

She waved her wand again and this time grass started to shoot up all over the platform.

'HEY!' shouted a train conductor, starting to walk towards us and waving his ticket machine about. 'What are you doing?'

'I'm just . . .' began Mum, but her words were drowned out by the sound of a train pulling up next to us.

'Come on everyone, quickly!' said Miss Cherry, hurriedly bundling everyone into the carriage. She pressed the button to shut the door before the train conductor could reach us.

Zoe pulled me towards a pair of
seats and we sat down as the train
started to move away from the station.
I felt a fizz of excitement to be inside
the huge clanking metal carriage.
Pink Rabbit and I stared out of the
window and watched as the houses
and trees rushed past at
lightning speed.

'It is almost like flying!' I said to Zoe. As we chatted and looked at the scenery, Miss Cherry walked up and down the carriage taking the register again.

'Just checking that everyone is on board,' she said.

Everyone was. Except Dad.

'Oh dear,' I said to Zoe. 'I thought Dad would have caught up with us by now. I guess he won't be coming after all.'

Just then Pink Rabbit began to fidget around on my lap, pointing with his paw out of the window. He had spotted something in the sky.

'What is it, Pink Rabbit?' I asked. 'What can you see?'

We peered up into the sky and squinted.

'It's a bird,' said Jasper. 'A big black bird with a bright pink tummy.'

'Hmm,' I said, squinting harder.
'I don't think it is a bird . . . I think . . .'

'It's your dad!' squealed Zoe. 'Your
dad's flying towards us!'

We watched as Dad soared closer, his vampire cape flowing out behind him. Vampires can fly very fast and it wasn't long before he was alongside the train, smiling in at the window.

'It's Isadora's dad!' screamed the class, all standing up in the carriage and pointing at him. 'Look!'

'Thank sugarplum fairies for that,' sighed Mum in relief.

'Oh my goodness!' said Miss Cherry with her hands clasped to her throat. 'That can't be safe!'

'Don't worry,' said Mum, leaning over and patting Miss Cherry's leg in a comforting sort of way. 'My husband is a very talented flyer.'

Dad continued to fly alongside the train until we stopped at the next station. Then he stepped into the carriage and flopped down onto one of the seats.

'Phew!' he said. 'That's my daily exercise completed!'

The class all cheered and Miss Cherry gave a frazzled smile.

Chapter THREE

When we got to the theatre I held onto Pink Rabbit's paw tightly. It was very crowded in the entrance. It made me feel all hot and prickly. There were so many people all jostling around and it was very noisy. We had to go and wait in a queue for a long time.

'Oh goodness!' said Mum, who is not

used to being in small crowded spaces. She waved her wand so that a cool gust of air billowed around us.

Dad was busy gazing at the posters of ballet dancers on the walls.

'Don't the men look suave!' he said, impressed. 'They are almost as sleek and well dressed as a vampire. That one even has a cape!'

'Everyone stay together,' called Miss Cherry, getting out her register again.

'I want to buy sweets,' said Bruno, pointing at a stand.

'Me too!' said Oliver. 'My mum gave me some money for food!'

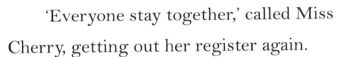

Once Miss Cherry had taken the register again we all scrambled towards the sweet stand. Mum gave me money to buy a packet of chocolate stars which are my favourite human sweets. Zoe bought some sour sherbet with her money.

'I think I shall have some strawberry laces,' announced Dad. 'They are the next best thing to red juice.'

Once we had all got our sweets, we followed Miss Cherry up some stairs and through a little dark door.

'Welcome to the theatre!' she said.

I felt my mouth drop open in amazement. We were in a *huge*, glittering auditorium. There were rows of velvet seats stretching all the way to the back and all the way up to the ceiling. At the front of the massive hall was a stage with a curtain across the front. Everything looked very fancy.

Miss Cherry led us towards a row of seats in the middle of the theatre and we all sat down.

'I can't wait to see the ballet dancers!' said Zoe.

'Me neither,' I said, popping a
chocolate star into my mouth. 'I especially
can't wait to see Tatiana Tutu! Nor can
Pink Rabbit.' I reached out to lift him onto
my lap so he could see the stage . . . but
I didn't feel any squashy pink paws . . .

I looked down.

Nothing.

My whole body went cold and my
skin started to prickle.

'Um,' I said, putting the bag of chocolate stars down and suddenly feeling very sick. 'Where's Pink Rabbit?'

Zoe frowned. 'Isn't he there?' she asked. 'You had him just before we bought our sweets.'

'I was holding his paw!' I said in panic. 'I must have let go of him when I was choosing the chocolate stars! He must have got lost in the crowd!' I stood up from my chair.

'I have to go and find him,' I said to Zoe. 'Poor Pink Rabbit will be so frightened.'

Quickly I made my way along the row towards Mum and the door that led back to the entrance.

'Where are you going?' asked Miss
Cherry as I approached. 'Isadora, sit
down, please. The show is going to start
in a minute.'

'I need to speak to my mum,' I said,
hurrying past her. 'It's an emergency!'

'What is it?' asked Mum when I reached her.

'It's Pink Rabbit!' I said in a panicked voice. 'He's gone!'

'Gone!' said Mum worriedly. 'What do you mean?' She stood up and took my hand. Together we made our way out of the auditorium.

The entrance foyer seemed very bright compared to the low light of the theatre hall, and it was quite empty now that most people had gone inside to find their seats. Mum and I scanned round for Pink Rabbit but we couldn't see him anywhere.

He wasn't by the sweet stand or by the toilets or by the counter where you hand in your ticket . . .

Where could he be?

We paced round and round the theatre foyer but he was nowhere to be seen.

'Pink Rabbit!' I called frantically, 'Pink Rabbit, where are you?'

'Maybe he's outside?' suggested
Mum. 'Let's have a look.'

We made our way out of the theatre
doors but my eyes were all blurry with
tears and I couldn't see where I was going.

'Sit down a minute,' said Mum,
giving me a hug. 'Don't worry, Isadora,
we'll find him. He can't have gone far.'

Together we sat down on the outdoor
steps and breathed in the cold winter air.
Mum wiped my eyes with a pink fairy
tissue that puffed sparkling dust all over
my face.

'Oops,' she said, 'wrong tissue.'

As we sat there I noticed a small door
a few metres down from the main theatre
entrance. Above it was a sign which read

I felt my hopes start to rise again.

'Mum, look!' I said, pointing. 'Do you
think that's where Pink Rabbit has got to?'

Mum looked doubtful.

'It's unlikely,' she said. 'That's the place where the actors and dancers go to get ready for the show. I don't see how Pink Rabbit could have got inside.'

'Maybe he got swept along with one of the dancers?' I said hopefully. 'I think we should check, just to be sure.'

'OK,' said Mum.

Together we flew to the door and pushed it open. It wasn't locked but there was a man sitting at a desk just inside.

'Hey!' he said. 'You can't come in here. This entrance is for performers only.'

'Oh dear,' said Mum, getting a bit flustered. 'Well, it's just that . . . well,

he's a pink rabbit, you see . . . he's very
special and he's only very little . . .'

As Mum gabbled a long story about
Pink Rabbit, I slipped quietly behind the
desk and into the room behind.

Unlike the bit inside the theatre where the audience go, it was not grand at all. Ahead was a long grey corridor with lots of doors on each side.

Some of the doors had names on but
I didn't stop to look properly. I tiptoed
silently past them all, past a clothes rail
of tutus, and a box of used ballet shoes,
down to the end of the corridor where
I turned a corner . . .

And there was Pink Rabbit!

He was standing alone in
the middle of the passage
and looking
very lost.

'Oh, Pink
Rabbit!' I said,
scooping him up into
my arms and giving
him an enormous hug.

'I thought you had disappeared forever! What happened? Did you get confused and follow the wrong people?'

Pink Rabbit nodded and nuzzled into my neck.

'Thank goodness I found you!' I said, putting him down. 'We had better get back to our seats now. We don't want to miss the show!'

We started walking back down the corridor, Pink Rabbit holding my hand, when a sudden sniffling noise made us stop. It was coming from behind the nearest door, the door with a big silver star on it, and it sounded very sad.

'Oh dear,' I whispered to Pink Rabbit.

'What shall we do?'

Pink Rabbit pointed towards the
exit with his squashy pink paw but
I shook my head.

'We can't just leave,' I whispered. 'Not if someone is upset. That's not a very kind thing to do. We should see if we can help.'

Pink Rabbit bounced back in alarm.

'Come on,' I said to him. 'Let's be brave.'

I lifted up my hand and knocked on the door. The snuffling sound from inside stopped immediately. After a minute or so the door opened, and a beautiful lady peeped out. I could only see her eyes but they were covered in silver glitter and she had on a pair of false eyelashes.

'Hello?' she sniffed.

'Hello,' I said in a small voice, suddenly feeling very shy. 'We just wondered . . . if you . . . if you were all right?'

The lady gave a watery smile and
blinked her huge eyelashes. Then she
opened the door a bit wider so we could see
her properly. She had a pair of white bunny
ears on her head and was wearing a white
leotard with a black velvet waistcoat.

She was also balancing on one leg.

'The White Rabbit!'

I gasped. 'Tatiana Tutu! It's you!'

'It is,' she said. 'I am Tatiana Tutu. But who are you?'

'I'm Isadora Moon,' I told her. 'And this is Pink Rabbit.'

Pink Rabbit put his paws behind his back and puffed out his chest importantly. Tatiana Tutu looked at him with interest for a moment and then she opened the door wider.

'Come in for a moment, won't you?' she said.

Pink Rabbit and I slipped inside the room and Tatiana Tutu closed the door.

I looked around and gasped in wonder.
The room was dazzling. There was a
big mirror on the wall with bright light
bulbs set around it, and from the ceiling
hung rows of sparkling tutus. On Tatiana
Tutu's dressing table was the famous star
diamond tiara.

'Wow,' I breathed, staring at it.
'It's so pretty.'

'You can try it on if you like,'
said Tatiana Tutu, picking it up and
putting it on my head. I stared into the
mirror and turned my head from side
to side, watching the diamonds flash
and twinkle in the light. My smile grew
wider and wider.

'It suits you!' laughed Tatiana Tutu. Then her face took on a more serious expression and I remembered why we were here. I took the tiara off and laid it carefully on the dressing table.

'Why were you crying?' I asked her.

Tatiana Tutu sighed and looked sad.

'I've hurt my leg,' she explained, pointing at the one she was holding up in the air. 'I tripped over on the way to the theatre. I thought it was going to be all right but it's hurting very badly. I'm not sure I can dance on it tonight and there's no time to get a replacement dancer now.

The show will have to be cancelled.'

'What?' I gasped.

'Yes.' Tatiana Tutu nodded, a tear trickling down her cheek. 'And it's all my fault, I've let everyone down.'

'Oh no!' I said. 'You can't help that you tripped. I trip over all the time! Is there no other way the show can go on?'

'Not really,' said Tatiana Tutu. 'You can't have *Alice in Wonderland* without the White Rabbit, can you?'

'I suppose not . . .' I said sadly.

'The other dancers are all so disappointed too,' continued Tatiana Tutu. 'That's why it's so quiet backstage right now. Usually everyone's hustling and bustling around and looking forward to the show. But now, it's like a ghost corridor!'

I nodded and Tatiana Tutu looked at the clock on her dressing-room wall.

'The show should have started by now,' she said. 'The stage director will have to go out very soon and announce that it's cancelled.' She wiped a tear from her glittery eye and sniffed.

'Oh dear,' I said. 'I wish I could think of something that would help.'

Pink Rabbit bounced up and down next to me and waved his paws in the air.

Tatiana Tutu and I both turned to look at him. He *grand jeté*'d across the room and did a perfect pirouette. He pointed his toes, just like a proper ballet dancer, and then gave a deep bow.

'Oh,' I said. 'Wait a minute! I think I have an idea . . .'

Chapter FOUR

Zoe stared worriedly at me when Mum
and I got back to my seat in the theatre.

'You didn't find him!' she said.
'Where's Pink Rabbit?'

'It's all right,' I told her, sitting back
down in my chair. 'I did find him but . . .
he's busy.'

'Busy?' said Zoe. 'What do you mean?'

'It's a surprise!' I said. 'You'll find out really soon!'

Zoe looked confused but she didn't ask any more questions. 'OK . . .' she said suspiciously.

We chattered quietly for a while longer but then the lights in the theatre went down and a great hush fell over the audience. The orchestra started to play and the great velvet curtain began to rise. Zoe and I breathed out in wonderment. The stage didn't look like a stage but a beautiful garden. In the middle was a tree with frothy pink cherry blossom all over it. The ballet dancer playing the part of Alice was sitting on one of the branches.

She was wearing a white tutu
with a black headband in her pale
blonde hair. Everything shone and
sparkled, and the cherry blossom
petals rained down from the tree.
The music suddenly got faster, and
the White Rabbit leapt on from
stage left.

Except it wasn't a *white* rabbit . . .

It was a little pink rabbit! My Pink
Rabbit!

He looked very small up there on the
stage and I suddenly felt very nervous for
him. But I also felt extremely proud.

Pink Rabbit tiptoed across the stage in his striped waistcoat. He was holding a pocket watch in his paw and looking at it as he leapt along.

'I'm late, I'm late, I'm late!' the music seemed to say.

Pink Rabbit bounced and bounded past the cherry-blossom tree and the dancer playing Alice jumped down and followed him. Together they danced round the pretend garden, twirling and soaring amongst the cherry-blossom petals.

'Isadora,' whispered Zoe. 'Is that . . . is that—?'

'Pink Rabbit!' I whispered back. 'Yes!'

'Wow!' breathed Zoe. 'He's amazing!'

We watched as Pink Rabbit did a
pirouette and then disappeared down a
pretend hole in the stage. Alice followed
him and everything on the stage began
to change. The tree vanished, the walls
and floor became black-and-white checks,
and suddenly Pink Rabbit and Alice were
falling down from the ceiling on strings.

Pink Rabbit didn't look frightened at all. He is used to flying through the air with me! He reached the ground and then elegantly danced off the stage, still glancing at the pocket watch.

The show continued and we watched the stage become transformed again and again. There was a magical forest with a giant caterpillar, and a garden of dazzling colourful flowers who all danced across the stage with Alice.

There was a tea party and a mad hatter
and a glittering pink stripy cat with a
huge grin. And, of course, there was Pink
Rabbit! He came dancing onto the stage
often, twirling and swirling and leaping
and bounding.

'That was magical!' said Zoe when
the curtain came down to show it was
time for the interval.

'It was!' I agreed.

The audience started to chatter
and people all around us began standing
up to go to the toilet and to get
refreshments.

'Did you see that little pink rabbit?'
I heard one man say behind me. 'He was

spectacular, wasn't he!'

'Yes,' said another man. 'I can't work out how they made him so small. It was like magic!'

'He was an excellent dancer,' said someone else. 'The star of the show!'

'And so original that he was pink,' said a lady nearby. 'Usually the Rabbit in *Alice in Wonderland* is white!'

I felt my mouth widen into a huge smile. Pink Rabbit had been spectacular and I was so proud.

Mum and Dad and all my friends began to gather round me then.

'Isadora,' Dad said. 'Was that really Pink Rabbit on the stage?'

'What was he doing there?'
asked Bruno.

'Yes, Isadora. How did it happen?'
said Sashi.

I tried my best to explain everything before the end of the interval. I was so busy explaining that I didn't even get to eat the little pot of strawberry ice cream that Miss Cherry had handed out to everyone.

'Wow!' said all my friends.

'Good for Pink Rabbit!' said Dad.

'I always knew he had a talent,' said Mum.

I stared round at them all and beamed.

The second half of the show was
a bit shorter. We watched as the stage
was transformed into more magical
wonderlands. Alice, Pink Rabbit, and the
other characters danced through them,
glittering and whirling in their brightly
coloured costumes.

At the end of the show all the
dancers came onto the stage. They
all bowed together and the audience
clapped and cheered. Then Alice made
a curtsey and the audience clapped and
cheered some more. Then I noticed
one of the dancers push Pink Rabbit
gently to the front of the stage.
He took his own bow and suddenly
the whole audience were on their feet,
stamping and whooping and cheering.
Mum waved her wand and a bouquet of
roses exploded in the air and fell down
around Pink Rabbit.

'Fantastic!' yelled the audience.
'He was magic!'

Pink Rabbit puffed out his chest
and I could tell he was extremely pleased.
He was pinker than ever!

Once the thick velvet curtain was lowered, the lights came back on in the theatre, and everyone stood up to go home.

'We need to wait for Pink Rabbit,' I said to Miss Cherry.

'Of course,' said Miss Cherry.

We had to wait quite a long time before Pink Rabbit appeared from backstage with a limping Tatiana Tutu.

'I'm sorry we took so long,' said Tatiana. 'Everyone wanted Pink Rabbit's autograph!' She smiled down at him. 'He was fantastic!' she said. 'The star of the show! We are so grateful to him. And also to you, Isadora, for lending him to us!'

She held out a box. It was wrapped in shiny paper and tied with a ribbon.

'It's a present for you to say thank you,' she explained. 'You and Pink Rabbit really saved the day!'

'Thank you!' I said, blushing.

'It's quite all right,' said Tatiana Tutu. Then she lifted her hand and waved goodbye to us all.

The train journey home seemed very slow. Pink Rabbit was tired after his day of dancing and he slept curled up in my lap for the whole journey. I wanted to open my present but Mum wouldn't let me. She squirrelled it away in her bag.

'Save it until you get home,' she said. 'It might seem unfair on the others.'

Zoe and I chatted about the show and looked out of the window at the darkening sky. Little flakes had started to fall. They looked like tiny twirling ballerinas.

'I hope I can be a ballerina one day,' I said dreamily.

'Me too,' said Zoe.

I looked down at Pink Rabbit sleeping peacefully on my knee and stroked his ears.

'It was wonderful to see him on stage today,' I said. 'I wouldn't change a thing about it. But . . . but . . . at the same time, I am a bit disappointed I never got to see Tatiana Tutu dance. I would have so loved to see her dancing.'

'I'm sure you will someday,' said
Zoe reassuringly.

It was dark by the time we got to the
station. We all walked back to the school
together and then my friends' parents
started arriving to pick them up.

'That's the last one!' said Dad, ticking a name off his clipboard.

'Excellent,' said Miss Cherry. 'Thank you so much for volunteering, Mr and Mrs Moon.'

'No problem at all,' said Dad cheerfully. 'It was an experience. I have never been on a human school trip before.'

'Nor have I,' said Mum, taking off her hi-vis jacket and handing it back to Miss Cherry. 'It was lovely to see the dancing. They looked almost like fairies!'

Dad seemed reluctant to take off his hi-vis jacket.

'I didn't realize I had to give it back,' he said disappointedly.

'I'm afraid so,' said Miss Cherry.
'It's school property.'

'I thought you hated it!' said Mum
in surprise.

'Well, it's rather grown
on me,' admitted Dad.
'It's a very striking look,
don't you think? I think
I will ask for one for
my birthday.'

★ ★ ★

Mum, Dad, and I flew
home through the snow,
picking up Honeyblossom
on the way.

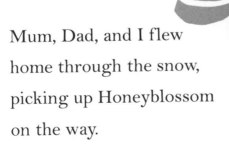

'Can I open the present now?' I asked eagerly as soon as we got in through the front door.

'Of course,' said Mum, handing it to me.

I let Pink Rabbit tear off the wrapping paper and then we peered into the box.

'WOW!!' I cried.

Tatiana Tutu's famous star diamond tiara winked up at me from a nest of pink tissue paper. I lifted it out carefully and put it on my head.

'Look!' I said to Mum and Dad. 'Look!'

'Oh my goodness!' said Mum. 'That is so beautiful.'

'How kind of Tatiana Tutu,' said Dad. 'It suits you, Isadora.'

Pink Rabbit continued to rustle in the box. When he came up he was wiggling his ears in delight and holding a set of tickets in his paws.

'Family tickets to Tatiana Tutu's next ballet show!' said Mum. 'You will get to see her dance after all!'

'Really?!' I said, a huge grin spreading over my face.

'Really,' said Dad.

I almost felt like crying because Tatiana Tutu had been so kind.

'I didn't do very much!' I said. 'All I did was knock on her door to see if she was all right, and then lend her Pink Rabbit for the show.'

'Well, it was still very kind of you,' said Mum. 'Not everyone would have done that. It may have seemed a small thing to you, but to Tatiana Tutu it was huge!

You saved the show.'

'It is always important to be kind,' said Dad. 'No matter how big or small.'

I nodded and Pink Rabbit nodded too.

'We will always try,' I said.

'Great,' said Dad. 'How about you be kind right now and fetch me some red juice from the fridge then? It's almost breakfast time and I'm starving!'

Are you more fairy or more vampire?

Take the quiz to find out!

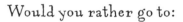

What's your favourite colour?

A. Pink   **B.** Black   **C.** I love them both!

Would you rather go to:

A. A glittery school that teaches magic, ballet, and making flowery crowns?

B. A spooky school that teaches gliding, bat training, and how to have the sleekest hair possible?

C. A school where everyone gets to be totally different and interesting?

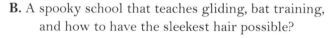

On your camping holiday, do you:

A. Put up your tent with a wave of your magic wand and go exploring?

B. Pop up your fold-out four-poster bed and avoid the sun?

C. Splash about in the sea and have a great time?

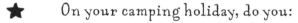

Results

Mostly As
You are a glittery, dancing fairy and you love nature!

Mostly Bs
You are a sleek, caped vampire and you love the night!

Mostly Cs
You are half fairy, half vampire and totally unique –
just like Isadora Moon!

Isadora Moon

Isadora Moon
Goes to School

Her mum is a fairy and her dad is a vampire
and she is a bit of both. She loves the night, bats,
and her black tutu, but she also loves the sunshine,
her magic wand, and Pink Rabbit.

When it's time for Isadora to start school
she's not sure where she belongs—fairy school
or vampire school?

Isadora Moon
Goes Camping

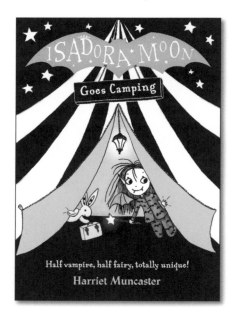

It is the first day back at school after the summer, and Isadora is called on to talk about her holidays at show-and-tell. She's worried. She had been to the seaside, like her friends, but strange things had happened there ... the sort of things that probably didn't happen on human holidays.

Isadora Moon
Has a Birthday

Her mum is a fairy and her dad is a vampire
and she is a bit of both. Isadora loves going to
human birthday parties, and now is going to
have one of her own!

But with her mum and dad organizing things, it's not
going to be like the parties she's been to before...

Harriet Muncaster

Harriet Muncaster, that's me! I'm the
author and illustrator of Isadora Moon.
Yes really! I love anything teeny tiny,
anything starry, and everything glittery.

Love Isadora Moon?
Why not try these too...

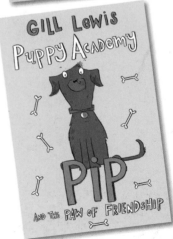